WHAT ABOUT AN OCTOPUS?

For my wonderful editor, Stacey Roderick, who loves
facts and octopuses just as much as I do —D.K.

To Miss Fong and Calef —D.L.

Text © 2024 Deborah Kerbel | Illustrations © 2024 Dawn Lo

All rights reserved. No part of this publication may be reproduced, stored in a retrieval system, or transmitted in any form or by any means, without the prior written permission of Owlkids Books Inc., or in the case of photocopying or other reprographic copying, a license from the Canadian Copyright Licensing Agency (Access Copyright). For an Access Copyright license, visit www.accesscopyright.ca or call toll-free to 1-800-893-5777.

Owlkids Books acknowledges the financial support of the Canada Council for the Arts, the Ontario Arts Council, the Government of Canada through the Canada Book Fund (CBF) and the Government of Ontario through the Ontario Creates Book Initiative for our publishing activities.

Owlkids Books gratefully acknowledges that our office in Toronto is located on the traditional territory of many nations, including the Mississaugas of the Credit, the Chippewa, the Wendat, the Anishinaabeg, and the Haudenosaunee Peoples.

Published in Canada by Owlkids Books Inc., 1 Eglinton Avenue East, Toronto, ON M4P 3A1
Published in the US by Owlkids Books Inc., 1700 Fourth Street, Berkeley, CA 94710

Library of Congress Control Number: 2023947793

Library and Archives Canada Cataloguing in Publication
Title: What about an octopus? : a fact-filled underwater adventure / Deborah Kerbel ; illustrations by Dawn Lo.
Names: Kerbel, Deborah, author. | Lo, Dawn, 1992– illustrator.
Identifiers: Canadiana 20230561039 | ISBN 9781771475716 (hardcover)
Subjects: LCSH: Octopuses—Juvenile literature. | LCGFT: Instructional and educational works. | LCGFT: Picture books.
Classification: LCC QL430.3.O2 K47 2024 | DDC j594/.56—dc23

Edited by Stacey Roderick | Designed by Elisa Gutiérrez

 Manufactured in Shenzhen, Guangdong, China, in February 2024, by C & C Offset
Job # HX6482

hc A B C D E F

 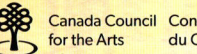 

 Publisher of Chirp, Chickadee and OWL
www.owlkidsbooks.com   Owlkids Books is a division of

Deborah Kerbel

WHAT ABOUT AN OCTOPUS?

A Fact-Filled Underwater Adventure

Illustrations by Dawn Lo

OWLKIDS BOOKS

Next time you visit the ocean, you'll want to look for seashells.

Oh, and what about an octopus?

When you do spot an octopus, you might be tempted to shake its hand. Please don't. A friendly wave is just fine.

Hello, Octopus!

FACT: All octopuses have eight arms. Some kinds of octopuses can detach an arm to help them escape when trapped or threatened. But don't worry, the arm will grow back. Octopuses are one of the very few animal species that can regrow parts of their bodies.

You'll want to give the octopus lots of space to swim around. Then when it gets tired from all that exercise, you can sing it a lullaby and wait for it to fall asleep.

FACT: Like humans, octopuses have two stages of sleep. For octopuses, the first is a quiet stage, when they remain very still and pale. The second is an active stage, when their skin darkens and their muscles twitch.

As its eyes start to close, it might reach for something soft to cuddle.

Octopuses are very sensitive.

FACT: Octopuses have two rows of up to 280 suckers lining each arm. The suckers are strong and sensitive. They are used for feeling, tasting, and gripping.

And when the octopus is finally asleep,
don't be surprised if it dreams about love.

FACT: Octopuses have three hearts. However, in their lifetime, most will choose only one mate.

When it wakes up, it'll be hungry and ready to grab breakfast.

With all those arms, it shouldn't take long.

FACT: Each arm of an octopus has its own mini-brain that controls its suckers individually, similar to the way we control our fingers. As a result, octopuses are excellent multitaskers.

As soon as its tummy is full, the octopus will most likely need to use the bathroom.

Don't worry if it sneaks away for some privacy. It will be back soon.

FACT: Octopuses are invertebrates, which means they have no skeletons. Their bodies are so soft and squishy, they can squeeze through small cracks and into tight spaces with ease.

Once it's finished washing up, it'll be ready for a game of tag.

You're it!

FACT: Octopuses are extremely smart animals. They've been known to figure out mazes, do tasks for rewards, and even play games.

You'll swim fast and come oh-so-close to catching the octopus.

But watch out! It might surprise you with a clever trick.

FACT: When an octopus wants to confuse a predator, it'll spray a cloud of ink and dart away.

So you'll give up and suggest a game of hide-and-seek instead.

At first, you'll probably come across lots of rocks, coral, and plants.

FACT: Octopuses can change the color of their skin. They can also change its texture to blend in with their surroundings perfectly. Whether they're hiding out on rocks, among coral, or in plants, octopuses can go from smooth to spiny in the blink of an eye. They're one of the few animals in the world that can pull off this trick.

You might even see some other animals. Some that are spiky. Some that are round. Some that are long.

None of them will look like an octopus.

FACT: The mimic octopus can bend and shape its body to mimic (or pretend to be) other animals. They can disguise themselves as jellyfish, flounder, sea snakes, and even sea stars!

Just when you're about to give up, you'll notice a pile of seashells.

Oh, that's right. Weren't you looking for seashells, too?

FACT: After dining on a meal of shellfish, octopuses make sure to clean up, often stacking the empty shells outside their den. This decorative pile of shells is known as an "octopus's garden."

You'll swim down to take a closer look. Hey, did that one just move?

Hello, Octopus!

FACT: When threatened by predators, octopuses have been known to cover themselves with shells to protect their soft bodies.

Goodbye, Octopus!

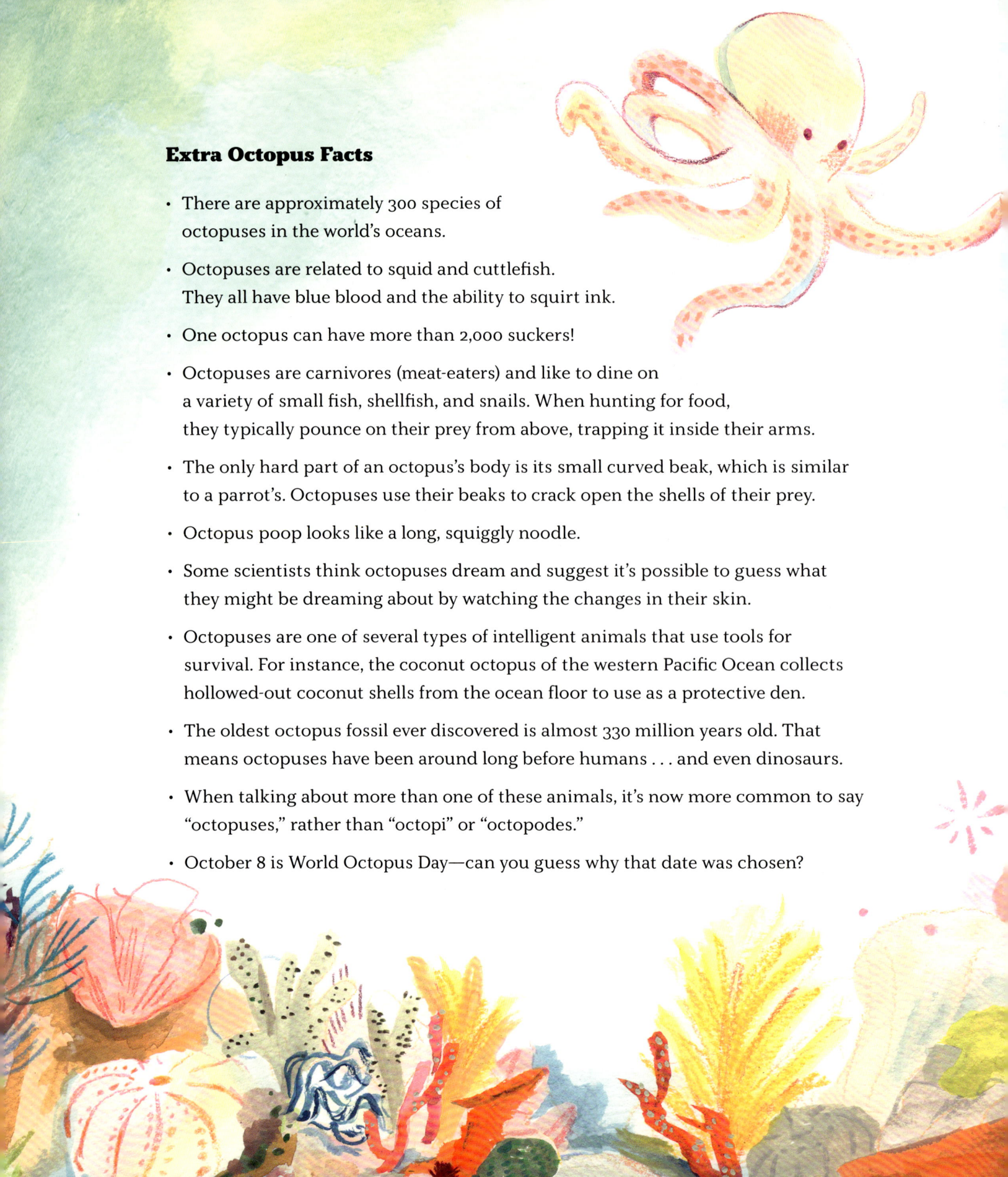

Extra Octopus Facts

- There are approximately 300 species of octopuses in the world's oceans.

- Octopuses are related to squid and cuttlefish. They all have blue blood and the ability to squirt ink.

- One octopus can have more than 2,000 suckers!

- Octopuses are carnivores (meat-eaters) and like to dine on a variety of small fish, shellfish, and snails. When hunting for food, they typically pounce on their prey from above, trapping it inside their arms.

- The only hard part of an octopus's body is its small curved beak, which is similar to a parrot's. Octopuses use their beaks to crack open the shells of their prey.

- Octopus poop looks like a long, squiggly noodle.

- Some scientists think octopuses dream and suggest it's possible to guess what they might be dreaming about by watching the changes in their skin.

- Octopuses are one of several types of intelligent animals that use tools for survival. For instance, the coconut octopus of the western Pacific Ocean collects hollowed-out coconut shells from the ocean floor to use as a protective den.

- The oldest octopus fossil ever discovered is almost 330 million years old. That means octopuses have been around long before humans . . . and even dinosaurs.

- When talking about more than one of these animals, it's now more common to say "octopuses," rather than "octopi" or "octopodes."

- October 8 is World Octopus Day—can you guess why that date was chosen?